ONE BRIDE & TWO GROOMS

A PRIDE & PREJUDICE NOVELLA

CHRISTIE CAPPS

Cover Design: SelfPubBookCovers.com/RLSather

For information on new Christie Capps releases and other news, please sign up for my newsletter at: jdawnking.com

Christie Capps is a pen name for Joy King, who also writes as J Dawn King.

She can be contacted on social media at:

Facebook: www.facebook.com/JDawnKing

Twitter: @JDawnKing

Email: jdawnking@gmail.com

For those who need a reason to smile

CHAPTER 1

"Miss Elizabeth Bennet, wilt thou have this man to be thy wedded husband, to live together after God's ordinance in the holy estate of Matrimony? Wilt thou obey him, and serve him, love, honor, and keep him, in sickness and in health; and, forsaking all other, keep thee only unto him, so long as ye both shall live?"

Before she could reply, the heavy wooden door slammed into the stones lining the entrance to Longbourn chapel. Silence fell over those gathered as they turned to see who dared to disturb the wedding.

"She will not," Mr. Fitzwilliam Darcy's rich baritone filled the silence. He was absolutely in no doubt of his opinion. He knew her as well as he knew himself.

The soles of his finely polished Hessians pounded down the aisle as he, master of Pemberley in Derbyshire, approached the bride and groom, the tails of his great coat billowing behind him. He knew he would be unwelcomed. He cared not. His purpose was not to make friends nor enjoy the celebration. As far as he was concerned, the marriage between Miss Elizabeth Bennet and her father's cousin, Mr. William Collins, was a travesty of epic proportions.

Mr. Bennet stood and moved alongside his second daughter. Her eldest sister serving as her attendant stepped back, distancing herself from the coming confrontation. The groom sputtered his confusion.

The bride's eyes captured and held Darcy's attention as he strode towards her. The lack of sparkle; the almost lifeless acceptance of her future tore at him. A trail of tears had already dried on her cheeks, giving evidence of her abhorrence at becoming Mrs. Collins.

Do not worry, my Elizabeth. I will rescue you.

Mr. Collins finally found his voice. "You cannot interfere, Mr. Darcy. Your betrothed, your own cousin Miss Anne de Bourgh would be appalled at your actions. Your soon to be mother-in-law, my esteemed patroness Lady Catherine de Bourgh, will hold you in disapprobation for interrupting a religious service."

"I am not betrothed." While Darcy knew it was the desire of his aunt that he marry Anne, he had never agreed to the match. Never! He was his own man, not subject to anyone other than Almighty God. "Neither should you be forward enough to attempt to attach yourself to this lady."

Mr. Collins grasped the lapels on his coat as his chest swelled in mock piety. "I comprehend your meaning, Mr. Darcy. I do know her position is inferior to mine.

However, I promised during my offer to never hold Miss Elizabeth's poverty against her. That I am heir to her family estate and the current clergyman of Hunsford parish elevates me to a status far above the Bennet family." Mr. Collins snorted. "By the by, the rector has already asked if any objected, and no one did. I am afraid, good sir, that you are too late. I will be taking Miss Elizabeth as a bride. She will reside in my house and share my bed. You have no business here." His smirk belied the simpering tone of his voice.

Darcy's eyes glanced at the parson only to find the toad's eyes leveled at Miss Elizabeth's chest as the disgusting man's tongue licked the drool from his lips.

Had they not been in a chapel, Darcy would have wrapped his fingers around the oaf's throat and squeezed.

"What is the meaning of this?" Mr. Bennet demanded, ignoring his wife's practiced swoon and the chortles of his youngest two daughters.

In the blink of an eye, Darcy bent and hefted the bride over his shoulder, quickly spinning to walk out the door. Three steps later, he turned back to Mr. Bennet. "She is marrying the wrong groom. She abhors him. She loves only me."

Less than twenty paces later, Darcy deposited her on top of Apollo then mounted the horse behind her. As he dug his heels into the flanks, a rush of spectators pushed through the door behind them. Within seconds, the escaping couple were out of the view of the crowd, the noise of Mr. Collins' yelling and Mrs. Bennet's wailing receding as Darcy and Miss Elizabeth galloped towards

Meryton. They were almost two miles on the other side of the small farming town when Darcy drew to a stop behind his most luxurious carriage. His bride deserved comfort for the long journey to Scotland.

His trunks were packed and loaded at the back. Miss Elizabeth's luggage had been picked up by Darcy's footmen. They were currently tied to his carriage, not that of the rented hackney obtained by Mr. Collins which had stood at the side of the chapel.

Thank heavens Longbourn's housekeeper was a sensible woman. Had she not been so, Darcy would have had to purchase clothing for his bride-to-be as they rushed to Gretna Green. They had no time to lose.

Without a word, Darcy tossed the reins to his groom and lifted Miss Elizabeth from the horse. Keeping her in his arms, he moved to the carriage only to have the door refuse to open. He pulled and pulled. To no avail. No matter how hard he yanked, the door would not budge.

Behind them, Mr. Collins, the remainder of the Bennet family, and the townspeople approached, holding cudgels, clubs, and torches—anger and determination on their faces.

Turning back to the carriage, he pulled with all his might. Nothing.

Yelling at his driver, Darcy tried and tried until the violent crowd was immediately behind them.

The first blow dropped him to his knees as Miss Elizabeth was pulled from his embrace.

"No!" he yelled. "No.....!"

* * *

"Sir?" Darcy's valet, Parker, pulled back the curtains to allow daylight to stream into his chambers. "Sir? I believe you were having a bad dream. Pray, wake up, Mr. Darcy."

"What?" Fragments of the nightmare continued to hold him in its grip. His hands quivered as he sat up and pressed his palms over his eyes. Leaning back against the headboard, he strove to clear his head.

"Mr. Darcy, you attended Mr. Bingley's ball last evening, retiring but four hours ago. Mr. Bingley will be leaving for London as soon as he wakes. You advised me to have your belongings packed to depart for Pemberley by nine this morning. It is now the eighth hour. Your bath is ready, and your traveling clothes are laid out in your dressing room. A tray has been ordered to break your fast. Is there anything else you desire, sir?"

"No, no." Darcy dropped his hands and looked around him as the autumn air chilled his sweat-soaked brow. The dream had felt real. So real that the vestiges of panic remained.

Confusion transformed into awareness of his surroundings and the events of the evening prior. Bingley's infernal ball.

Miss Elizabeth Bennet had opened the gathering by dancing the first set with Mr. Collins. The man had no business on the dance floor. He could not follow even the simplest of patterns. Darcy worried for Miss Elizabeth's toes as the parson repeatedly turned the wrong way.

Before the music had completely stopped, she stepped away from her father's cousin to seek the company of Miss Charlotte Lucas, a sensible woman in Darcy's opinion. He had watched Miss Elizabeth the rest of the night. Although Mr. Collins approached her for the final dance, she refused to stand up with him. Miss Elizabeth would not be leaving any of her neighbors with the idea she was in any way attached to the parson.

However, in the clear light of morning, the salient point was why in the world *he* was upset about whether or not the country miss had intentions towards Mr. Collins or not. It meant...she meant...nothing to Darcy.

Or, did she?

Perhaps he had overindulged in drink. Counting back, Darcy had consumed only two glasses of punch. The trace of alcohol in each cup was not enough to bring on such a fantastical vision. Surely!

What was it that had Darcy's sub-conscious thinking of her as a potential bride? She had only a small portion, her connections were almost non-existent, and the conduct of the majority of her family was reproachful.

He was a Darcy, grandson of an earl with a family name that went back a multitude of generations. He was proud of his heritage—his noble lineage.

Ah, he remembered. The reminder filled his chest with heat and his mind with wonder.

She was a lady like no other of his acquaintance. Miss Elizabeth was lovely, kind, loyal, and intelligent enough he could foresee decades of interesting discussions should they be in company. Her happy countenance and pleasing manners would make it a joy to have her at his side. And, those eyes...brilliant orbs holding the wisdom of the ages.

Running his palm over the scratchy morning growth

on his chin, Darcy pondered his own circumstances. He was proud of his accomplishments in the five years since his father died, increasing Pemberley's coffers as he tended to the Darcy investments and properties. He knew his place in the highest circles of society. He bore his family name well.

Despite appearing to have it all in the eyes of others, what he lacked was a companion who would fill Pemberley with laughter, who would share the challenges of daily life, and who would care for him. He saw clearly the benefits of having a capable mate.

What he did not want was a wife who desired Darcy for what he *had* rather than the man he *was* inside. Miss Elizabeth had never once appeared to have been impressed with his wealth or his position in society.

Darcy had ordered Parker to pack for removal to Pemberley, which was to avoid attaching himself to her. He had felt the danger of her. Yet, now that he knew Mr. Collin's intent, the simple truth was that Darcy simply could not leave.

During a brief conversation between sets, the parson had boldly stated his purpose of being in Hertfordshire. He had been commanded by his patroness to attach himself to one of the Bennet daughters. Mr. Collins had selected Miss Elizabeth for the position of wife. When Darcy had asked if the young lady had accepted him, Mr. Collins confessed he had not yet made his offer nor received approval from her father. This horrid breach of propriety, where Mr. Bennet's cousin had given Darcy leave to believe it was a foregone conclusion, left Darcy more determined than ever to stop this travesty. Darcy could not ... would not accept vibrant, lively Miss Elizabeth becoming wife to a man lacking in appreciation for her wonderful qualities.

Had the parson been such a wolf as Darcy's nightmare had portrayed him? Certainly. Many times during the ball, Darcy had noted the direction of the ingrate's gaze. In fact, he doubted the clergyman could state with accuracy the color of Miss Elizabeth's eyes but could measure within an inch the dimensions of her chest.

Disgusting that a man of the cloth lacked self-control!

Throwing the bedclothes back, Darcy stood with a purpose. Likely, Mr. Collins would rise early to make his proposal to Miss Elizabeth. Should Mrs. Bennet have her way, the offer would be accepted as it would guarantee her personal security after the death of her husband. Mr. Bennet's response was unknown. The relationship between him and his second child appeared close. Nonetheless, that did not necessarily make the support of his daughter's happiness his paramount concern.

Darcy could not take the chance that Miss Elizabeth's parents would believe this would be the only opportunity for their daughter to marry.

The impropriety of barging in on someone else's offer of marriage in an attempt to stop the proposal would not be a barrier to Darcy. This was a matter of halting an injustice against a worthy young woman.

"Parker, I have changed my mind. I shall remain in Hertfordshire another se'nnight. I have an important task to perform as soon as I am readied." Moving quickly towards the dressing room, Darcy stripped off his linen nightshirt and stepped into the bath.

What was he about? Was he thinking his dream had been reality? Certainly, it was not. Never could he imagine Miss Elizabeth willingly allowing her person to be tossed over his shoulder like a sack of potatoes on the back of a merchant. Her independent nature would have had her kicking and pummeling him with her small fists in the insistence that she was more than capable of walking on her own. Nor would she have kept silent during the whole ordeal as she had done in his nightmare. Her tongue would have ripped strips of flesh from his back as easily as a whip.

He chuckled to himself. Would he like to hear her view of his dream-state actions? Oh, yes.

For a certainty, had the dream been real, Mrs. Bennet would have been grateful for his reported ten thousand a year income in comparison to the annual salary of a parson. Despite Mr. Collins being heir to Longbourn, he would never be able to see to the needs of a widow and four dependents should Mr. Bennet die, even if he were so inclined. Most likely, the matron would have knocked Mr. Collins from in front of the altar to see Darcy take his place. Perhaps Darcy should have sought her assistance? Hah!

And, Mr. Bennet himself? His indolence was well-reported upon. Nothing Darcy had learned in the six weeks he had been neighbor to the Bennet's estate indicated Mr. Bennet would rouse himself for his family's behalf. Would he have done anything to stop Darcy from eloping with his daughter? If Darcy had read the man's character correctly, surely, he would not.

Once dressed, Darcy requested Apollo be brought around. He had an important call to make that could no longer be delayed.

CHAPTER 2

His suppositions about Mr. Bennet were gravely in error.

By the time Darcy arrived at the neighboring estate, the master of Longbourn had already broken his fast and was relaxing in his study. When Darcy was shown into the room, Mr. Bennet was slow to rise, setting his book aside with apparent difficulty.

"To what do I owe the honor, Mr. Darcy?" Due to the early hour, tea was not expected. However, it was ordered. "Pray do not wait until the amenities have been seen to, sir. I keenly anticipate learning of your purpose in arriving well before visiting hours."

His comment unsettled Darcy. His expectation of welcome by a man of inferior circumstances coupled with the remnants of the dream left him unable to utter the words he had practiced on the three-mile trip from Netherfield Park.

Swallowing, Darcy's mind cleared.

"Last evening, your cousin declared himself betrothed to Miss Elizabeth, your second daughter."

"I know who she is," although his brows lifted, there was no amusement in Mr. Bennet's tone.

"Pardon me for my seeming interference in your family's business, but I do have a purpose..."

"Which I am waiting to hear." Mr. Bennet sat forward, resting his arms on his desk. The knuckles on his fingers were white.

Clearing his throat, Darcy said, "I cannot believe you, as her father, would not appreciate the unevenness of a marriage between Mr. Collins and Miss Elizabeth. He is a dull man unduly impressed with his patroness who happens to be my own aunt. Lady Catherine uses her exalted rank to justify interference in every aspect of the lives of those under her authority. She would find your daughter's wit to be impertinent. I can only imagine the discord there would be in the Collins' household. He would bow to my aunt's authority and would demand the same of his wife. My aunt would remain unchanged while Miss Elizabeth would struggle under the pressure of her demands."

"I see." Mr. Bennet unclenched his fists. "I thank you for your opinion. Nonetheless, I still am unclear as to why you are bringing this to my attention. Do you care so much about the feelings of your own relative that you decided to step forward to interfere with mine?"

Darcy sighed in frustration. This was not how he had imagined the morning.

"No, sir." Standing, he moved to the window. From

there he saw that Mr. Bennet had a clear view of who arrived and departed Longbourn. Deciding he had nothing to lose, Darcy turned back to the man.

"In the six weeks since I was first in company with Miss Elizabeth, I have come to realize that she would make me a good wife. In truth, I have much more to offer than Mr. Collins. My estate, Pemberley, is one of the finest in the nation, and my income..."

Mr. Bennet lifted his hand to stop him.

"Pray, take a seat, Mr. Darcy." Mr. Bennet stood and gestured towards the leather chair Darcy had sat in when he first arrived. "I have a few questions for you before you continue."

Walking to the front of the desk, he leaned back and crossed his arms.

"Mr. Darcy, are you, indeed, speaking of the same young lady you proclaimed in public in the hearing of herself and her neighbors to be merely 'tolerable and not handsome enough to tempt you' as well as 'a punishment for you to stand up with'?"

"She heard?" Horror at his rudeness shook him to his toes.

"She did." Mr. Bennet smirked. "In addition, while she stayed at Netherfield to care for Jane, Elizabeth reported that she was often verbally attacked by Miss Bingley in an effort to elevate said lady while denigrating my family. According to Lizzy, not once did anyone rise to her defense except Mr. Bingley. Not once, Mr. Darcy. Since you were often in the room, your silence implies your own guilt at believing these attacks to be accurate."

He gulped as the truth of Mr. Bennet's words flooded him with feelings unknown to him. To be grouped with Bingley's pernicious sisters was terrible. He personally disdained them both. Mr. Bennet was correct. His silence gave tacit support to their propensity to make themselves look better by insulting those they felt were not of their social sphere.

"In addition, ..."

Lord, was he not done yet?

"In addition," Mr. Bennet's words were clipped, as if each syllable was weighty in itself, "my own observation of your dance with my daughter at the ball proved she holds you in derision. Tell me, sir, as the words flew back and forth between you two, did you at any time think you held the upper hand? I cannot imagine so as you stomped away, leaving her standing in the middle of the floor without escort until my cousin, the man you treated with disapprobation and have spoken of with disdain this morning, helped her to her mother."

"I... I," Darcy rubbed his hands over his face. *Was this another nightmare? Was he, somehow, reliving the past six weeks while gazing at his own actions and attitudes in a mirror?* Impossible! He was a Darcy. His position was in the first circles. He was welcomed by the finest hostesses in town. The *ton* was his playground should he want it, which he did not.

This man! This man, who presumed to castigate him for...

Darcy's outrage was gone in an instant. What of anything Mr. Bennet had said was not true?

Swallowing again, he endeavored to explain.

"I cannot...I..." He tried again. "I perfectly comprehend your feelings." Darcy wanted to vomit. "As the guardian of my young sister, had any man come to me with an interest in her who had acted in the manner you perceive me to have done, I would have cut him directly, ending any hopes he had of attaching himself to my family."

"Do you believe I should do less with mine?" Mr. Bennet asked, his jaw as stiff as his shoulders. The man was livid. "I know who you are, Mr. Darcy. I know your uncle is an earl. My wife informed me of your income the night of your first public appearance. I also know who I am. More importantly, I know my daughter." He thrust his index finger at Darcy. "I know without a doubt that she has no tender feelings for you at all. Neither does she for Collins. Both Lizzy and Jane will marry only when they can hold their potential mate in respect and affection. I care not if they are a prince or a pauper, sir. The happiness of my children, especially my eldest two, is paramount to me."

Mr. Bennet stood and returned to his seat. "You have misjudged both my daughter and me, Mr. Darcy, in fundamentals a fool would find obvious. I cannot imagine you consider yourself as a lesser man to a fool?"

"I do not!" Darcy stood. Anger at the truth of Mr. Bennet's words warred with his ire against the gentleman. *How dare Mr. Bennet address him in this manner?* Never had he been treated with this level of disrespect. Not since Wickham... *Blast!*

George Wickham had once been his closest friend.

During their university years, Wickham took on the personality and vices of those miscreants he selected as his companions. By the time Darcy inherited at his good father's death, there was no healing the former friendship of the two men.

In the years since, Wickham had pressed and coerced Darcy using threats of rumors and harm to gain his way. Because of this, Wickham no longer feared the master of Pemberley, going as far as to attempt eloping with fifteen-year-old Georgiana Darcy in an effort to gain her large dowry and revenge himself on Darcy.

Despite the passing of four months since the attempted elopement was discovered, Wickham flagrantly spoke against Darcy, telling one lie after another to gain sympathy with the hearer and cause animosity against either Darcy.

Obviously, Wickham's presence in the neighborhood for the past two weeks had not been idle. He had used his time to his personal advantage.

"Mr. Bennet, last night during the time I danced with Miss Elizabeth, she mentioned the suffering I caused Mr. George Wickham. Are you aware of his accounts against me?"

"I believe he has told his tale to anyone who would listen." Mr. Bennet lifted a brow.

Darcy understood his curiosity. Wickham appeared a distant transition from his own seeming insulting behavior.

"Perhaps I should start at the beginning, Mr. Bennet, so there is no longer any confusion to complicate matters." He asked for the conversation to be kept between the two of them.

Upon the older man's agreement, in as few words as possible, Darcy outlined his history with George Wickham, including the attempted elopement.

"My sister has yet to recover her spirits, Mr. Bennet. The day of the Meryton Assembly, which I had not desired to attend, I had received a heartbreaking letter from Georgiana whereupon she clearly expressed her failures. However, the failure was solely mine. I, who knew the sort of man Wickham was, kept her in ignorance due to her tender years. Never had I imagined the level of deceit he was capable of promulgating against someone he at one time treated as a little sister."

"In addition, Miss Caroline Bingley, who desires to become the next Mistress of Pemberley, had attempted to arrange matters that same day to promote a match—with me. She knows how much I despise being the center of attention, how much I loathe having my worth equated solely with my income, so offered to remain behind at Netherfield with me while the others went to the assembly. This I found unacceptable. During each turn of the wheel from the time we left Bingley's estate until our arrival in Meryton, we were subject to her opinions of what a degradation it would be to enjoy country company. Thus, I was tired, irritated, frustrated, and heartsick, Mr. Bennet. I had no desire to dance with someone whose mother screeched mine and Bingley's income every few minutes. I have no doubt Mrs. Bennet would have paired me with Miss Elizabeth should I have offered to stand up with her for the set. I have no doubt any mother of an unattached daughter would have done the same, so please do not take insult with my comment about your wife. She is, as is every mother in the *ton,* concerned with attaching their offspring to the most eligible gentlemen possible. I hold no grudge against her or any of them."

"Mr. Darcy!" A familiar twinkle lit Mr. Bennet's eye, similar to the one he had seen each time Miss Elizabeth attempted to give him a set-down. "Can you speak even a few sentences without insult? I cannot believe an educated man of the world with as much to offer as you believe you have does not know how to temper his comments with tact. Or, is the quality completely foreign to you?"

"I apologize, sir," Darcy offered in an attempt to sue for peace. "I would like to continue if you would bear with me."

"Pray, just tell me your purpose. That is all I ask."

"I want to marry Miss Elizabeth."

"You do?"

It was then Darcy saw a hint of a smile.

"Do you believe she would be agreeable?" Mr. Bennet's smile grew.

"As you have reviewed her version of our exchanges, I do not," Darcy admitted. "Nevertheless, you should know that I have fought a personal battle against my expectations, my family's, and society over the past few weeks. Miss Elizabeth first intrigued me, then impressed me as I witnessed her loyal care of her sister plus her kindness to those beneath her as she asked for assistance during that care. Her intelligence as we engaged in debates, and her beauty have since set her apart as being the only woman of my acquaintance I could see spending a lifetime with."

Darcy continued, "I have much ground I need to cover to gain her good opinion, Mr. Bennet. I am willing to do whatever it takes to help her, and you, see that I am a man of honor and duty worthy of respect and admiration. I will humble myself, if need be. I will do anything within my power to have her want to be my bride."

At Mr. Bennet's nod, Darcy continued, "When Mr. Collins told me last night that he was already betrothed to Miss Elizabeth, I determined first that the man was presumptuous in his claims, and second, I would use every asset I have available to see she would not have a lifetime of unhappiness because of an unequal marriage to him."

"I am happy my cousin was of service," snorted Mr. Bennet.

"Sir, I cannot accept you would be pleased with a match between your daughter and your cousin. Although I do discern the value of him as your heir, I need to remind you of the opportunities I could provide your family in excess of Mr. Collin's ability."

As Mr. Bennet opened his mouth to respond, the door to his study flew open. Elizabeth burst in, closely followed by Mrs. Bennet and Mr. Collins. All three were speaking at once.

"I will not marry him. Papa, do not make me accept him, I pray you."

"Mr. Bennet, you must make our silly daughter marry Mr. Collins."

"Sir, you must talk some sense into Miss Elizabeth.

She is acting the demur debutante. I will not have it. Lady Catherine will not have it. Mine will likely be the only offer she will ever receive. She must marry me."

Mr. Bennet yelled, "Silence!"

Into the quiet he spoke. "We have a guest."

CHAPTER 3

"Mr. Darcy!" all three interlopers observed at the same time.

"Yes, Mr. Darcy has arrived this morning on a mission of some interest to our family," Mr. Bennet responded.

"Ten thousand a year," Mrs. Bennet said, barely under her breath.

"Lizzy, Mr. Collins, you may remain. Mrs. Bennet, I ask that you rouse the rest of our daughters to break their fast before evening falls. I will discuss the outcome of the coming discussion with you later today."

Obediently, Mrs. Bennet left the room. To say Darcy was stunned at her doing so would have been a serious understatement. He had thought he understood her character as meddlesome. Then again, he had thought he had a clear comprehension of Miss Elizabeth's desires. He had been wrong.

Mr. Bennet had Miss Elizabeth sit between the two men as he, again, took his seat. She crossed her arms, then her legs, refusing to look anywhere but at her father.

"Let us begin this discussion with some information." Turning to his cousin, he asked, "How long were you in the drawing room while you made your offer?"

"But a few moments," was Mr. Collins' immediate reply.

"Three quarters of an hour," from Elizabeth.

If Darcy had thought Mr. Bennet was angry before, the hue of red that covered his face from chin to hairline indicated his ire was far vaster than when the man displayed it against him.

"You were behind closed doors alone with my daughter for that length of time? What do you mean by this?" Mr. Bennet demanded.

"I..." the clergyman stuttered. "I had many reasons for marrying that I needed to discuss with my intended. Lady Catherine said..."

"Enough!" Mr. Bennet's voice reverberated from the walls. "I care not for Lady Catherine's opinion. The salient point is that your inept attempt at a marriage proposal put my daughter's reputation in danger. Shame on you! As a man of the cloth you should know better."

Mr. Collins responded quickly, "Since, as you have pointed out, I have compromised Miss Elizabeth, I will marry her as soon as the banns can be called."

"Over my dead body," Darcy said under his breath.

Apparently, both Miss Elizabeth and Mr. Bennet heard. Her head spun towards him. Mr. Bennet's brows rose until they almost disappeared.

Miss Elizabeth opened her mouth to speak. Darcy had no doubt her words would be scathing.

"Lizzy, before you say anything, I need to inform you

that there has been another offer for your hand in marriage." Mr. Bennet glared at Mr. Collins. Looking at Mr. Darcy, he asked, "Does the fact that she was alone with Mr. Collins for a considerable length of time dissuade you from your decision?"

"It does not."

"Then, the fair thing to do is to allow you the same amount of time to state your case." As Darcy nodded, pleased at the arrangement, Mr. Bennet continued, "I will not subject my daughter to further censure by your secluding yourselves from oversight as Mr. Collins did. Knowing Lizzy's desire to enjoy nature, you shall walk exactly twenty-two and one-half minutes from Longbourn towards Meryton, at which point you will turn and walk back for the same time period. Have no doubt, Mr. Darcy, and you too, Lizzy, that not only will you be in my purview, I would guarantee my wife will be in the front room window watching as will my remaining daughters from their windows upstairs. There will be no improper conduct. Am I understood?"

"Yes, sir."

"But, Papa..." Elizabeth made another attempt to gain her father's attention.

Mr. Bennet stopped her again. Looking at Darcy, he asked, "Have you a time piece?"

"I do."

"As do I." Mr. Bennet removed the gold piece from his pocket. "Gather your things, Lizzy. Your time starts as soon as I hear the front door close behind you."

"But..." Mr. Collins and Miss Elizabeth said in unison.

"Mr. Collins, for justice to be served, for the remaining

se'nnight of your stay at Longbourn, you shall have thirty well-chaperoned minutes a day to convince my daughter of your intentions. Mr. Darcy will have the same." Mr. Bennet pushed himself back from his desk to stand. "I highly suggest you either write to your Lady Catherine for her suggestions or you spend time alone pondering how you might impress the woman you claim to hold in affection."

The confidence of Mr. Collins was unbelievable. Darcy wanted to laugh aloud at his next comment.

"I shall spend my time wisely. I shall choose to be unconcerned about Mr. Darcy's appeal for Miss Elizabeth's affections. He is betrothed to his cousin, Miss Anne de Bourgh. Thus, he cannot marry another. As well, taking seven days to court my fair lady, her love will increase by suspense, according to the usual practice of elegant females." He had winked at Miss Elizabeth when he stated the last.

As in the dream, Darcy wanted to wrap his hands around the man's throat and squeeze.

Mr. Bennet interrupted Darcy's joyous imaginations.

"Mr. Collins, you had best get busy. Mr. Darcy and Lizzy shall be walking out. It will be up to Mr. Darcy to explain clearly his relationship with Miss de Bourgh." To his daughter, "Lizzy, get your bonnet." To Darcy, he said, "Mr. Darcy, I would advise you to think before you speak." Again, he stopped his daughter from commenting or, rather, complaining. "Be off with you all."

Mr. Collins led the procession, abandoning them to gather his thoughts. Darcy waited while Miss Elizabeth donned her pelisse, bonnet, and gloves, grumbling under her breath the whole time. Her attempts to address her father with a refusal for both potential grooms had been in vain. Mr. Bennet lifted his book and pretended to read.

When the front door closed behind them, Darcy checked his time piece, noting the minute, second, and hour. It would not do to be late. He was on his honor.

Within seconds, it did not look well for Darcy. When he offered his arm, Miss Elizabeth looked at him like he was a warty bullfrog. Stepping away from him, she began walking, shoulders back, her arms stiff at her side, with her gaze straight ahead.

He was in deep trouble.

Reminding himself of the nightmare, the ridiculousness of the parson, and the fact that he did, indeed, desire her for his wife, Darcy hurried to catch up.

"Miss Elizabeth, we must have some conversation."

As soon as the final word left his mouth, he recalled it was exactly the same as her taunt at the ball.

"Must we?"

"Your father's intents and my purpose demand it to be so," he unwisely replied.

"Demand?" She halted and turned on him, her hands now fisted, and her chin thrust forward. However, it was in her eyes where he saw the true danger. They were not limpid pools of loveliness. Instead, they were blazing.

He felt as if his hair might ignite under her gaze.

"By what reason do you feel you can demand anything of me, sir. I cannot imagine you would want anything to do with me at all. Your prior comments, your continuous staring at me to find fault have not endeared you to me in any way. Therefore, these forty-five minutes are a waste of my time."

How much humiliation could he stand? Competing with an oaf like Mr. Collins for the hand of a lady who disdained him. What was he about?

"I like you." It was the only thing that, in his confusion, came out of his mouth. "Please believe me, I was not looking at you to find fault at all. In truth, you intrigued me. I am still intrigued."

She scoffed.

"Miss Elizabeth, pray listen." He slowed his pace, hoping she would do the same. "If someone gave you a wrapped package the size, shape, and weight of a book, would you assume it was a book inside?"

She looked at him quizzically, slowing her pace until he caught up with her. "I would."

"What if it was the size and shape, but not the weight? Would you still be confident with what was inside?"

"No, I would not."

"Neither would I." He paused to gather his thoughts. "Each of us, both you and I, has taken the measure of each other. With that said, the simple truth is that we have only observed what is on the outside. Yes, we have drawn conclusions, some correct and some not. But until we unwrap the paper, we cannot be for certain what is contained within, correct?"

"Yes, I can see how that would be." She adorably put one finger to her chin. "Are you implying I do not know the real Mr. Fitzwilliam Darcy and that you do not know the correct version of me?"

"That is exactly what I am saying." He stopped. So did

she. "I have explained my poor attitude the night we met at the assembly to your father. Gratefully, he accepted the extenuating circumstances behind my rudeness. Now, I beg for your forgiveness for uttering a lie in your presence. You are far more than tolerable and are certainly handsome enough to tempt me. As a gentleman, I should never have had such thoughts about a female. My shame is only exceeded by my embarrassment at having been overheard. I failed to act the gentleman."

She gave no quarter. "You did."

"Your father also reminded me to clarify my relationship with my cousin Anne. Never have I wanted to marry her, and she has never wanted to be my bride. Only her mother sees the benefit of our being joined in matrimony. Lady Catherine's reasons are purely selfish. With Anne as my wife in distant Derbyshire, Lady Catherine could keep control of her estate in Kent. I have never proposed to anyone in my lifetime."

She nodded, accepting his explanation. Then it hit him. He was wrong.

"Oh, my word! Forgive me," he begged. "I just told another lie. I, for whom honesty is a part of my very being."

He no longer could look upon her lovely face, such was his remorse.

"I did ask Anne to marry me," he confessed. "I was eight-years-old. She had a pony I wanted to ride. She was two years older and had never learned to share. She refused me in no uncertain terms. I lost a bride and an opportunity to ride her horse with one word. I was far more devastated about the animal than the girl."

"I see."

There was not one note of teasing from her, nor humor at his tale.

"Miss Elizabeth," he sighed, removed his beaver hat, and ran his hand through his hair. "While I had assumed you would expect my address, your father assured me you did not. It was apparent from the response you gave when you entered your father's study that Mr. Collins' addresses were not warranted nor appreciated either. Neither your father, Mr. Collins, nor I have allowed you to have your say about the events of last night at the ball and this morning in Mr. Bennet's study. You have tempered your opinions under great duress, I am sure. Perhaps the better way to start is for you to speak your mind." He stepped back from her, bowed, and indicated with a sweep of his arms that she had the floor.

CHAPTER 4

Her words hit him with the force of a tornado.

"I loathe you as equally as I do Mr. Collins, sir." Elizabeth glared at him as she spoke. "Other than a few essentials, you and Mr. Collins are very much the same. Your pompous superiority, your officious opinions, your slighting of my family and my neighbors should make you question your definition of what a true gentleman is."

She barely took a breath before continuing. "In comparison, I look to the example of amiable Mr. Bingley and charming Mr. Wickham." She smirked. "Oh, I see your reaction at the mention of his name. It is no different than it was during our dance. When given the opportunity to clarify your relationship, you responded with pithy comments that did nothing to inform me as to the man's true character, which reflects poorly upon yours. Is this the mark of a true gentleman? I think not."

"You, Mr. Darcy, have misused your wealth and family name to trample upon the kind citizens of Hertfordshire who wanted nothing more than to welcome you to the area. You belittled my family, treating my own mother as if she was a bug you would enjoy squashing each time you are in the same room. The mask of indifference you wear fails to hide the disapprobation in your eyes when you are in her company. Is this the mark of a true gentleman? Absolutely not."

"When Miss Bingley and her supercilious sister made condescending cuts against me and the sweetest lady on the planet, my dear sister, Jane, you did and said nothing," Elizabeth snorted. "No, that is not entirely correct, is it? Despite my intention not to eavesdrop, I could not help but overhear your slight when I removed myself from the drawing room. At Miss Bingley's comment, 'Eliza Bennet is one of those young ladies who seek to recommend themselves to the other sex by undervaluing their own, and with many men, I dare say, it succeeds. But, in my opinion, it is a paltry device, a very mean art.' And, do you recall your response, Mr. Darcy?"

When he started to answer, she added, "Oh, do not struggle to remember, sir. You clearly said, 'Undoubtedly'. Is this the comment of a gentleman? No."

"Just as Mr. Collins cared not for my opinions or feelings, completely disregarding any response I made to him, you too have never really listened to what I had to say. You have continued in your sole pursuit of your own happiness, unconcerned about the happiness of others, in particular, of mine. Is this selfish disdain for the feelings of others the mark of a true gentleman? Of course not."

"Lastly, I watched you closely when Jane and Mr. Bingley were in company. Your blatant disapproval was as obvious on your face as if you had penned your feelings on parchment and shared it with the room. How dare you judge my sister as wanting in any way. She is reticent in company, yet completely relaxed around your friend. Did you note that, sir? Of course, you did not. Why? Because you cannot look beyond your own exalted conclusions. Jane is very much like the wrapped package you mentioned. Her serenity hides deep feelings. She carefully and wisely guards her trust. In my opinion, she has no peer. Yet, you overlook her worth because she lacks wealth, connections, and is not overt in displaying her feelings. How could you? Do you feel you have been overt in displaying yours?"

Tears born of anger filled her eyes. He felt wretched at his actions having caused them.

"Mr. Darcy, the only reason I can assume that you would want me for a bride is an unhealthy desire to lord your circumstances over one much lower in society. Does it make you feel more the man when you do this? Does this somehow feed your ego? Is your arrogance and conceit not enough that you need to keep someone downtrodden so you feel good about yourself? I cannot begin to imagine any other reason why you have spoken with my father this morning. You certainly never indicated by your actions or speech that you held me in affection. I definitely do not have kindly feelings towards you at all. Thus, to press your suit is repellant to me to the same extent I felt when Mr. Collins attempted to gain my consent this morning."

Elizabeth paced back and forth twice until she stopped before him. "Am I clear in all I have said? Is there any ambiguity I need to interpret or simplify so there is no doubt in your mind or mine that you fully comprehend my feelings?" She taunted him, her ire as vicious as each word she uttered.

"No, Madam. I fully understand your feelings and your reasoning," he said.

With a heart crushed and battered, he bowed to her, checked his time piece, and turned back towards Longbourn. "It is time we return."

In silence they walked the lane leading to the front door. Mr. Bennet had been correct. His wife was waving a white handkerchief from the window of the front room, and a series of changing female faces peered out the upstairs glass. Mr. Collins paced back and forth in front of the door, effectively blocking their way.

"I will see you inside to the safety of your father," Darcy offered.

Miss Elizabeth tipped her head slightly in acceptance.

IT WAS a weary and beaten Fitzwilliam Darcy who rode Apollo recklessly through the fields between Longbourn and Netherfield Park. With Bingley in London, Darcy sought to avoid the company of Miss Bingley and Mrs. Hurst. Even Mr. Hurst, Bingley's brother-in-law, would not have been good company. Or rather, Darcy knew he himself would be a poor companion to anyone.

No, I will not become maudlin! Darcy mused. *I will not allow sorrow to overtake me from the results of the morning. I will not wallow in self-pity. I will not allow Mr. Collins to win!*

He needed help. Realizing he had dug himself into a hole so deep he could no longer see daylight, Darcy pondered who best could advise him. Certainly not his closest friend, his unmarried cousin, Colonel Fitzwilliam. The man lacked tact, could charm the ink off a page, and had never loved anyone or anything more than his horse.

Returning to Netherfield Park, he handed Apollo to a groom and hurried to his chambers. There he dipped his quill into the ink and wrote.

30 October 1811

Netherfield Park

Dearest Georgiana,

I hope this finds you well. Before you ask, yes, I did dance at Bingley's ball. Regretfully so.

My dear sister, I find I am in sore need of some assistance and believe you are the perfect person to solicit for help. In asking this of you, I pray you will understand that I am not wanting to harm your tender sensitivities by reminding you of the unsavory event of this summer. However, from our discussions I sense that romance has been very much on your mind. I also understand that you now discern the difference between infatuation and true love.

I cannot invite you to Hertfordshire as that rake who exposed himself to you as ungentlemanly is in residence not three miles from Bingley's estate. I would never place your person in his path. Therefore, I beg you to consider the following carefully before you give me the fullness of your youthful wisdom on paper if not in person. Pray forgive me for my errors which you will read below. I offer no excuses for my poor conduct except my feet have been swept out from under me by a lady your size, if you can imagine. It is to regain my footing that I seek your help.

Her name is Miss Elizabeth Bennet. She is without equal. For a certainty, she is not the bride I ever expected to marry, as she has no fortune nor position in society. Yet, she is delightful.

There is another who seeks her as his wife. He has far less that he can offer her. Nonetheless, Miss Elizabeth is far from mercenary. She would not choose me because of Pemberley. Thus, I am left with only my character to impress her. In this, both myself and the other man have failed astronomically.

You see, at first, I believed her to be beneath my notice. Her father is a country squire with a silly wife and a total of five daughters. Where Miss Elizabeth and her elder sister are not avaricious, their mother very much is. I had assumed, incorrectly, that all the daughters, including Miss Elizabeth, were like the matron of the family.

Upon becoming better acquainted, I failed to take into account the negative aspects of being in the company of Bingley's sisters when in Miss Elizabeth's presence. While, for the most part, I ignored their snide comments, Miss Elizabeth believed my silence to be agreement with the sly remarks that were, in truth, insulting. In addition, Wickham's presence in the area with his tales of woe against my person has created a vast gulf between me and the lady I admire. She finds Wickham charming, as you can imagine.

I have been offered by her intelligent father the opportunity of having thirty minutes a day for the next six days to convince Miss Elizabeth that my suit is superior to the other man's. Since she will not marry without respect and admiration, I am direly in need of quickly improving her opinion of me so she can see clear to accept me as her husband.

This no doubt has distressed you, dear Georgie. I apologize for discomposing you. I need to know: How do I please a woman worthy of being pleased?

Pray give this careful consideration, but do not take too long. The clock is ticking until I meet her again. I would feel more confident if I had your sound guidance accompanying me when I arrive at Longbourn in the morning.

I am always your

Devoted brother,

FD

Sealing the missive, he had Parker take it directly to Meryton to engage an express rider. If all went well, the letter would be in Georgiana's hands in the late afternoon. Hopefully, he should have a reply before morning. In the meantime, he prayed for divine intervention. He needed all of the help he could get.

CHAPTER 5

Bingley returned from London late that evening. Darcy was pacing impatiently when he walked into the library.

"I stopped by Darcy House to see if they had correspondence needing your attention." Bingley grinned at the huge stack of mail in his hands. "I continue to be grateful this falls to your lot and not to me. By the by, Miss Darcy asked that I personally deliver this one to you along with a message that a longer reply will be sent express before daybreak in the morning."

Darcy yearned to rip the parchment from the hands of a friend who had only ever been kind to him. Instead, taking the time to ask about the success of Bingley's business, he was ill-prepared for the length of Bingley's reply.

Finally, he held the letter. Excusing himself, Darcy rushed to his room. Prepared to welcome Georgiana's fount of female perception, he broke the seal to find only four words. Four small words that had the power to weaken his knees until he dropped into a chair.

Beads of perspiration gathered on his upper lip as he crumpled the paper in his hands— hands that shook. *Oh, Lord!* What was he going to do now?

Smoothing the parchment over his thigh, he reread the words that were now indelibly imprinted in his soul. *"Do you love her?"*

How was he to answer? Did he, indeed, love Elizabeth Bennet?

He was ready and willing to make a fool of himself in her pursuit, was he not? Was that not love? Or, was it merely the competition that had stirred him to action? Was it the idea of her attached to Collins that motivated him?

Darcy's mind began to play horrendous tricks on him.

He closed his eyes to ponder Georgiana's question. Immediately a picture appeared of Mr. Collins alone with Elizabeth in a carriage, he dressed in his parson's black, she garbed in the same dress she had worn to the ceremony in the dream that started his preoccupation with marrying Miss Elizabeth. As soon as the newly wedded Collins' transport pulled away from Longbourn, Mr. Collins boldly moved to sit alongside his new bride. Taking her hand in his, he pulled her towards him for a lengthy...

No! Standing, Darcy poured himself a brandy, drinking it in one gulp. Walking to the window, he pulled aside the curtains to look out at the black of night. Another picture filled his vision. Elizabeth, for she was now Elizabeth to him, dressed in black from under her chin to her toes. It was not Collins who had died. Instead, it was her laid out for public inspection by those who genuinely cared for her. Reports whispered amongst the mourners were that she had died of a heart broken by disappointments and sheer boredom.

Wanting to bawl, Darcy stiffened his spine. The pain of loss from that last vision hit him in the gut, twisting and pulling until he felt he could not take in the next breath. His thoughts churned with the same pulsing rhythm until he felt he would be sick.

Returning to the chair, Darcy kept his eyes open as he reflected on the condition of his heart. Would he have missed her had he left for Pemberley early that morning? Would he have regretted not seeing her again? Would he have forgotten her in a few weeks? Could there be someone else out in the world he had yet to meet who had better circumstances, had the same ready intelligence, and the same soulful eyes?

Shaking his head, Darcy had no more need to ponder when the answer was as obvious as the nose on his face. He well and truly loved Elizabeth Bennet with a heartfelt affection that robbed him of any ability to look elsewhere. She, and only she, would complete him. Where he lacked, she had strength. Where he was more than adequate, she...no, she was insufficient in nothing.

Reading Georgiana's note again, he knew his answer with confidence. He, Fitzwilliam Darcy, master of Pemberley and Darcy House, was madly in love with Miss Elizabeth Bennet.

He smiled. The relief at having reached the proper conclusion relaxed him. He knew exactly what he had to do. Strategize. He would plan his offensive in detail, so he missed nothing. The war was on. Darcy was determined to be the victor. However, first, he needed to make a defensive maneuver. He would write to her the full extent of his dealings with Wickham. In that way, he would not need to use his thirty minutes to explain the truth about the rogue. Instead, he would court the lady properly.

WHILE HE WAITED for Georgiana's full response, he rode Apollo over Bingley's fields looking for wildflowers. Somehow, he inherently knew Elizabeth would prefer them to hothouse roses. Unfortunately, the seasonably chilly weather of the past two mornings plus the downpour they had each of the four days preceding Bingley's ball had destroyed any hopes of his presenting her a lovely bouquet. He did see some pretty leaves but chose not to gather them as a gift. What was he to do?

Returning to Netherfield after his exhaustive search, he arrived at the same time as the express delivery. When the young man pulled a lone letter from his pouch, Darcy approached in hopes it was for him. It was.

Before he could gather a few coins from the purse from his pocket, the rider lifted out a wrapped bundle.

"This be for you as well."

Darcy hefted it in his hands. It was weighty. *What could Georgiana have sent?*

Thanking the man for his service, Darcy pointed him towards the servants' entrance so the young man could get a meal and respite before he left for his next stop.

"The person what arranged the delivery asked that I wait for your reply should you have one."

Darcy nodded, then left him to rush to his rooms. On his way inside the house, Darcy told the butler he wanted to remain undisturbed.

Hesitating, he wondered whether to read the letter first or open the package. Letter.

30 October 1811, late evening

Darcy House, London

Dear Fitzwilliam,

Thank you for your letter. I will admit to some surprise at your handing me the task of assisting you in winning Miss Elizabeth. Although I will not expect you to take the time now to write me in detail, I would like to hear much more about her. She sounds, as you said, delightful.

Due to my lack of experience, I considered what would be the height of romance to me. This is a dangerous thing to do, as I am too young to be thinking in this manner. However, with your permission, I would ask that you think about my reply with all seriousness.

First, one of the greatest treasures you can offer a woman is to beg her opinion, listen to her reply carefully, then heed her advice. Most often, females are ignored or considered ignorant in every matter other than running a household or performing those accomplishments expected by the ton. To be paid attention to is a rare treat and would set the man apart from all others.

Second, another treasure is to offer some of your private self to her. This shows you trust her. Trust me, dear brother, this increases the respect a female has for a man.

Third, and this is related to the last, is if she were to share a private thought with you. Cherish it, Fitzwilliam. For a lady to do so to a gentleman is a rare gem.

Finally, consider what interests you hold in common. Make this the subject of your discourse.

Pray, beware of offering false compliments or an excess of compliments. Instead of making a lady feel pleasure, it worries her that you only see what is on the outside of her, rather than her actual self. In truth, I fell victim to Wickham's ploys as he showered me with little, practiced praise. Upon reflection, it proved his disrespect for me.

As you realize, I have enclosed in a separate package several gifts I believe your Miss Elizabeth would appreciate. This was, by far, the most challenging aspect to this task. I first needed to consider the sort of lady who would touch your heart. Please use them as you see fit, or not.

Wishing you success as you seek to please your lady's heart.

Your devoted sister (who would love a sister of her own),

GD

Pulling at the string until it broke, Darcy unwrapped her offerings. Perfect! He would use each and every one of them. *Bless you, Georgie!*

* * *

DARCY HAD DECIDED to wait until visiting hours before arriving at Longbourn. It was his hope Mr. Collins had already used his thirty minutes. He had.

It was a ruffled, irritated Elizabeth who greeted him in her father's study.

Before they left for their walk down the lane, he addressed Mr. Bennet.

"Sir, I ask your permission to provide Miss Elizabeth an explanation of my dealings with George Wickham in written form. Should you feel the need to read my repetition of yesterday's conversation, I will leave it with you as we walk."

After indicating he had no desire to read the letter, Mr. Bennet pulled his watch from his pocket. "As a reminder, your time begins with the closing of the front door. You will be within my eyesight for the full thirty minutes. I suggest you use them wisely."

Handing the parchment to Elizabeth, Darcy watched as her finger ran over the lettering of her name on the front before she laid it back on her father's desk. "I shall read it when we return."

Once she had her outerwear on, he checked his time piece as the front door closed. Again, he offered his arm. Again, he was rejected.

"Miss Elizabeth, might I inquire after your morning?"

She harrumphed.

"I see. Apparently, your interview with my competition did not go well."

She rolled her eyes but still remained silent.

"Then I will offer you a token sent by my sister for you rather than conversation." He worried he was acting too quickly. At the tilt of her head towards him, he was encouraged to continue.

From his inside pocket he pulled a white linen handkerchief with three small daisies embroidered in one corner. A simple loop pattern of some sort was woven around the edges of the cloth. He had seen far more elegantly fashioned handkerchiefs than this one, but the daisies were a wonderful touch—a simple piece of nature that conjured up summer strolls and picnics.

"This is lovely." Elizabeth's thumb rubbed gently over the flowers. "I love daisies. They are a happy flower." She looked at him directly, a small grin on her face. "Pray, do thank her for me."

"I will," he said as he stretched out his arm towards the lane. "Should we continue?"

At her nod, they again started walking. "Might I suggest for the next twenty-four minutes that we quietly enjoy our surroundings—finding peace amidst the autumn day?"

"Please, Mr. Darcy. I would like that more than all else."

"Then, lead the way. I will gladly match my stride to yours." He gazed down upon her, wishing she would turn her face his way so he could see more than the side of her bonnet. However, he would not ask.

He did see the corner of her mouth tip up. She was smiling.

Vowing to be true to his word, he said nothing as they strolled the country lane between the trees. The turning of the leaves to yellows, oranges, and reds appealed to the senses. The crisp air somehow soothed him. Or, was it his companion?

Occasionally he checked his watch. At the allotted time, they turned around like dancers moving to the same rhythm.

When they were a few minutes from the house, she finally spoke.

"Thank you for your consideration, sir. I will not reveal the machinations of Mr. Collins to you as that would hardly be fair. Nevertheless, I will share that the half hour spent in your company was surprisingly refreshing. Again, I thank you."

After a slight curtsey, she entered the house, leaving him on the front steps.

He was joyous! He had never had a courtship before, and he had done well. What a difference twenty-four hours had made. He could not wipe the smile from his face the whole way back to Netherfield Park. Deciding to avoid company, he again went to his chambers to plot and plan for the next day. After the success of the morning, how difficult could it be?

CHAPTER 6

How wrong he had been. Within two minutes of being in Elizabeth's company the next morning, he knew his confidence had been misplaced. He knew the exact time, as he had checked his watch.

"Sir, as is the way with sisters, I placed your gift and letter on the side table in my chambers where I suspect it was Lydia who happened upon them. Deciding she needed the handkerchief more than I did, she placed it carelessly in her pocket."

"Did she not realize it belonged to you?" he asked innocently.

"If it was indeed Lydia, she was fully aware the gift was mine. Her propensity to freely 'borrow' ribbons and such is known to all of us in the family." Elizabeth took several steps before continuing. Her tone became sharp. "Needless to say, she was just as careless with your gift as she was in respecting my possessions. She must have shown the handkerchief to my mother."

"I see." He truly did not see. "Did your mother not like

the pattern Georgiana affixed to the corner?"

"Mr. Darcy," she huffed. "You do not see at all."

Four more steps went by before, gratefully, she clarified.

"My mother, who is determined Mr. Collins shall prevail in this courtship contest, immediately absconded with the linen to show Mr. Collins. Therefore, this morning, I was gifted by him a package filled with yards of uncut cotton, skeins of the gaudiest colors of yarn, and needles the length and thickness of which I have never used before, nor ever will."

"I see." This time he really did comprehend her vexation. Not once when she took care of her sister at Netherfield did he see her pick up a needlework project to work on. "I take it that sewing is not your preferred means of spending your spare time?"

"No, it is not. But that is not the point." She stopped. Using her index finger, she poked him in the chest. "Because of you, I now have in my possession enough fabric to clothe all five of us females in undergarments for the next several years. The yarn is thick and heavy, quite inappropriate for anything other than darning a man's wool stockings. The colors Mr. Collins chose would need to be hidden at the bottom of the stocking by leather boots. The needles could be used in a sword fight with my worst enemy who, at this point, is definitely *you!*"

Although his inclination was to laugh aloud, Darcy mustered control of his expression.

"Worst enemy seems rather harsh for a gift of that nature, Miss Elizabeth."

"You truly do not understand." She flapped her arms

and harrumphed. Poking him again, this time much harder than the last, she explained, "I despise needless needlework, Mr. Darcy. I would much rather fill my time with a good book, a sewing project that would be beneficial to someone in need, or good conversation. Now, I will be required to soothe Mr. Collins' ego and my mother's demands by spending hours in pointless activity using materials I would not have chosen in my lifetime. Do you now understand my situation?"

"You poor soul." He could no longer contain himself. Laughter burst from him into the stillness of the day. When she smacked him on the chest with her hand, he clasped it to him, then moved it to the crook of his elbow.

Walking on, he looked to see her response when he regained control. Her smile lit the autumn day brighter than the sun. Boldly, he moved a bit closer to her as they strolled down the lane.

"Miss Elizabeth, I see I shall need to reconsider today's gift."

"You brought another gift, sir?" She chuckled. "I do hope it is not poetry or I will be spending thirty miserable minutes tomorrow after breaking my fast listening to Mr. Collins' version of an ode to stir my affections towards him. I simply will not have it, Mr. Darcy."

He could not keep a blush from creeping up his neck. Indeed, a small volume of Shakespeare's sonnets was already in his coat pocket. It was Georgiana's second gift she had sent. This particular book was precious, as the bookplate attached inside was addressed to Lady Anne Darcy from his father. It was given with love on the first anniversary of their wedding.

"Sir, are you well?"

There was nothing for him to do except pull the sonnets from his pocket and hand them to her.

"Oh!"

"Yes, oh." He sighed. "This was also sent by my sister. She genuinely believes that if left solely up to me, I will fail in my attempts at romancing a worthy woman. Georgiana desires my happiness as much as I desire hers."

"That was very kind of her. Nonetheless, I was serious about not accepting gifts, especially if they are not coming directly from you. For I will become better acquainted with your sister than you. I believe that would defeat the purpose of the few days we have remaining."

Blast! Now, what was he to do? He returned the book to his pocket after accepting it back from her. Looking at his watch, he found it was time to return to Longbourn.

"Miss Elizabeth, if you would accept the following, I would be appreciative." He stopped before turning back. Bowing, he placed his hand over his heart and recited, gazing into her eyes through the entire sonnet:

"Let me not to the marriage of true minds
Admit impediments. Love is not love
Which alters when it alteration finds,
Or bends with the remover to remove:
O, no! it is an ever-fixed mark,
That looks on tempests and is never shaken;
It is the star to every wandering bark,
Whose worth's unknown, although his height be taken.
Love's not Time's fool, though rosy lips and cheeks
Within his bending sickle's compass come;
Love alters not with his brief hours and weeks,

But bears it out even to the edge of doom.
If this be error, and upon me prov'd,
I never writ, nor no man ever lov'd."

"Unfair!" she exclaimed, looking away from him. When she imitated his stance, putting her hand over her own heart, he was almost undone.

Some message, a universal truth, passed between them until Darcy realized he would never view her the same as he had done before the recitation.

"Mr. Darcy, we must speak of something other than poetry, I pray you. For, I am unprepared for the power of the Bard's words spoken with such feeling."

He grinned, but only to himself. He had been romantic! His chest began to swell with pride when something she had mentioned earlier stopped him in his place.

"Miss Elizabeth, you mentioned that Miss Lydia found both the handkerchief and my letter. Pray, tell me she did not read its contents." Blind panic flooded his chest until all tender emotions vanished.

"Be at ease, sir," Elizabeth started walking back to Longbourn. "She did not."

"Did you?"

"Yes, every word."

He silently waited for more. Elizabeth had never failed to express her opinions freely in front of him, so he was surprised she withheld her impressions now. He began to be uncomfortable. They were nearing the dreaded front door.

His palms began to sweat. The letter exposed Wickham's sins, Georgiana's almost elopement, and his own indolence at allowing Wickham to get away with his crimes. It was not until he had completed the four pages and reread what he had written that he realized how culpable he had been. There was no honor in allowing others to be hurt. Going behind Wickham and cleaning up after the rake was admirable to a point. Yet, stopping the cur in the first place should have been done years ago. If he recognized how bad the missive made him look, Elizabeth's sharp mind would have immediately known the same.

Although the letter did not advance his suit with the lady, it had to be done.

"You are too kind to trifle with my feelings," he began. "If, because of my disinclination to take Wickham to task you would reject me, pray, let me know now. I will depart Hertfordshire to never return."

He held his breath. It had not been his intention when he opened his mouth to leave her with an ultimatum. It was too soon. His courtship had been less than one hour. Half of that had been spent in pleasant silence.

"No, do not let me know. Instead, please forget I said what I did."

Kindly, she asked, "Would you, then, explain yourself?"

"Yes, thank you." He inhaled deeply. "From your comments at the ball, I understood you had been captivated by Wickham's many charms. Few are able to resist him. My account of his activities and proclivities had to hurt you if you did not believe my words to be true. To an innocent, as you are, my charges would appear like the vilest slander against a favorite. They could be perceived to sprout from bitter jealousy that he is far more capable of making friends than I. If this is your situation, Miss Elizabeth, I offer my sincerest apologies."

"Do not, sir." Elizabeth swallowed. "When I started with the first page, I was angry. At you. Where he had acted the gentleman, you had not. Thus, it was almost an insult against all I stood for to find out my ability to sketch a character, my perceptions and opinions, were flawed far more than anything I had mentally accused you of being."

She closed her eyes and took a deep breath. "Is Miss Darcy well?"

"She is...recovering her trust slowly."

"I would ask, and pray forgive my impertinence, which of the Bennet daughters, myself included, is your sister most like?" Tilting her face up to him, he saw the turmoil in her eyes.

"She is gentle and quiet like your eldest sister, a great reader like you, and as concerned about ribbons and lace as your youngest, I believe."

"I see." Elizabeth rested her index finger on her chin. "The accounts about her are exceedingly unequal."

"How so?" It angered him to find others freely spoke about his sister.

"From Mr. Bingley's sisters, I understood Miss Darcy to be a paragon of accomplishments and grace; far too serious in her achievements to be concerned about a simple country miss like myself. Mr. Wickham described her as proud and arrogant." She stopped when he sucked in a breath. "However, she cared enough for a stranger to send me daisies. That speaks more of my Jane than the rest of us girls. Thus, I believe Miss Bingley does not truly know your sister's character and Mr. Wickham used his comments to fuel my hatred of you."

He had no idea how to respond. Therefore, he said nothing. He was grateful when she continued.

"Sir, when my father told me two days ago that I had to accept thirty minutes from Mr. Collins and thirty minutes of company from you, I was beyond upset. I felt it was penance and I had done nothing deserving of such treatment." She shook her head at herself. "Now, I discern his wisdom, for not only am I coming to know both of you gentlemen better, I am coming to know myself as well. I am not happy with my father's interference, my mother's pushing Mr. Collins at me like he is my final hope, and the arrogant beginning you had in my company. However, I do appreciate the opportunity to become more self-aware. This will service to benefit me in the future, I believe."

She took the last few steps to the door. "Because of this, I fully accept your letter as truth."

The air left him in a noisy huff as relief gave birth to a seed of hope.

She reached for the handle before he thought to move.

"Sir, did you speak to my father of all you wrote in your letter? Has he been warned about Mr. Wickham's character?"

"Yes, he knows all the details in full."

"Then, I do hope one or the other of you will act quickly to protect the good citizens of Meryton, especially my younger sisters." She dipped in a small curtsey. "Good day."

With that, she was gone.

CHAPTER 7

When he returned to Netherfield Park, Bingley was waiting for him. Darcy would have been unsurprised had his friend taken him to task for being absent as Darcy knew he had been a poor guest.

"Darcy, the express rider has been busy. You have another letter and a small package from Darcy House." Bingley offered them into Darcy's willing hands. "By the by, would you want to go over the estate books this afternoon? I am willing if you are."

"Actually, I have an important conversation to hold with Colonel Forster. One of his militia men is unworthy of the uniform. Instead of withholding proof, which I have in abundance, I am honor bound to reveal him for the miscreant he is before too much damage to the community is done. As the primary landowner in the county, I would appreciate your company while I complete my errand."

Bingley stood taller for being asked.

Within a short while, the men rode towards the

encampment. By hour's end, Mr. George Wickham was under arrest. Sixty long minutes later, Darcy and Bingley returned to Netherfield Park. Darcy was poorer for having settled Wickham's outstanding accounts, but richer for doing what he should have done years prior.

During the time they were gone, the letter from Georgiana was not far from his mind. He spent the afternoon with Bingley and the estate books, then retired to his chambers to see what his sister had sent.

Holding the opened parchment on his lap, he opened the gilded box. *Ah, perfection!* He could not wait until the morrow.

* * *

"THERE IS a spy in my house, Mr. Darcy, and I am uncertain which culprit bears guilt." Elizabeth was in no better mood to start their walk than she had been the prior three days. "Somehow, Mr. Collins found out about the poetry. Deciding he could improve on Shakespeare's sonnet 116, he read to me from Fordyce's Sermons for the complete thirty minutes." She huffed. "In an attempt to gain favor, he offered to read an extra half of an hour so I would not need to 'tolerate your presence'—and I quote."

Darcy wanted to chuckle and probably would have had it not been slightly unmanly.

"I am pleased to see you convinced Mr. Collins of the unfairness of his offer." He bowed, checked his time piece, and offered his arm. This time, she accepted. Darcy felt like the victor already. Yet, he knew he risked being knocked off his high horse, a medieval term used when only the wealthy could afford a tall animal. He had plenty of tall stallions and geldings in his stables. What he did not have was the confidence that he was finally winning Elizabeth's approbation.

"Have you heard from Miss Darcy since yesterday? I cannot believe she would eavesdrop and gossip like my sisters must. I can only imagine it was either Kitty or Lydia."

"I did receive a letter and package from her yesterday afternoon. They were both intended for you. However, you did tell me not to bring any more gifts, and I would hate to be accused of being unfair despite Mr. Collins' attempts to cut me out of my well-deserved time."

"What? You left my gift from Miss Darcy at Netherfield Park?"

He wanted to laugh. She looked seconds away from plunging her hands into his great coat pockets to see what he had brought. He loved her curiosity. And her joy.

"Very well, I shall let you see her note."

Taking the folded parchment from his pocket, he opened it and handed it to her so she would not need to remove her gloved fingers from his arm.

"What is this?" Pointing to Georgiana's brief letter, she demanded in no uncertain terms. "Where is it?"

"Hah! Now it is you who does not play fair, Miss Elizabeth." Stopping, he dug into his outer pocket for the gilded box. Georgiana's brief one-sentence message had read, "Sweets for your sweet."

Elizabeth held the small container in both of her hands. Removing her gloves, giving them to him to hold, she opened the lid to find two elegantly decorated pieces of chocolate-covered marzipan.

They took her breath away. Her hand flew to her chest and she stopped breathing. He was so pleased he decided then and there to give the whole of his fortune to Georgiana. Deservedly so. Well, not the whole bulk of his wealth. He would owe her for the rest of his life for this one perfect moment in time.

Carefully, Elizabeth lifted one of the candies. Turning it this way and that, she surveyed every bit of sweetness before sniffing the rich chocolate coating. Delicately, she bit off one end.

Gulping, he imagined his face turned beet red and then as pale as the Dover cliffs. He watched her lips surround the treat. *Oh, Lord! Was he going to survive this intense jolt through his body at her actions?*

"Mmm!" Her eyes closed as she savored the taste. "This is the best thing I have ever tasted."

He gulped again, repeatedly. Barely able to breathe, he accepted the box with the remaining piece as she wrapped her fingers tightly around his elbow and started down the lane.

"Yummmm...!" she moaned.

He about fainted—not that men fainted, of course.

"I have never...oh, please give my sincerest appreciation to Miss Darcy. She is a queen, is she not?" When she finished the first piece and licked her fingers...beads of sweat broke out on every surface of his body.

"And, if I eat them both before we return to Longbourn then it is not as if I was bringing a gift inside for Mr. Collins to see, is it?"

He found his voice.

"We are of like mind, my lady. Enjoy your 'sweets for my sweet' and I will tell you more about Georgiana, if it pleases you."

She reached for the second piece to savor exactly as she had done the first candy. Before she took the first taste, she replied, "I would be very pleased."

THEIR THIRTY MINUTES flew by as quickly as a lightning bolt travels across the sky. He spoke not only about his sister, he also told Elizabeth about growing up at Pemberley, the close relationship between his father and mother, and how lonely he had been when away at school.

"I hope to one day show you Pemberley. There is no doubt in my mind that the abundance of books in the library along with the many lovely walking paths will delight you."

She smiled up at him without answering. Before he knew it, they were back at the door. As he was searching for the words to say a proper goodbye, Mr. Bennet popped his head out the door.

"Mr. Darcy, I see your courting is going as to plan." His bushy eyebrows wriggled mischievously. "Mrs. Bennet requests the honor of your company as well as that of your hosts at Netherfield Park for a meal tomorrow after church. Whether or not you have thirty minutes to walk out remains to be seen. It looks like rain. Shall I tell her you accept her invitation for yourself and your party?"

Darcy finally looked away from Elizabeth to see heavy

clouds gathering. Yes, they would be in for a good soaking. Accepting the invitation, Darcy could not resist asking, "Sir, when you refer to my courtship going as planned, are you considering your plans or mine?"

His only response was a hearty laugh as Mr. Bennet opened the door further to allow his daughter entrance. Before he closed it shut, Mr. Bennet said, "We shall see, shall we not? Mr. Collins returns to Kent early Wednesday morning. My Lizzy has three choices I have placed in front of her. Mr. Collins. You. Or, no one. Her decision shall be made by then. Goodbye."

At that, Darcy was left standing alone on the front steps.

Three days. He only had ninety minutes total to make a favorable impression with the lady. A momentary panic rose inside him which he tamped down. He needed a clear head to plan his next move. And, he needed Georgiana.

* * *

THE NEXT MORNING, the only one in the breakfast room early was Bingley. Giving attention to his host was a pleasure for Darcy. There were few men of his acquaintance with such purity of heart.

"Darcy, I have hardly seen you a minute since the ball. My sisters have commented that they, too, are disappointed at not having your company. Thus, it is a pleasure we shall spend the morning in worship, the afternoon meal with the Bennet family, and this evening here at Netherfield."

"I apologize, Bingley, for my inattention." He seated

himself across from his friend. "I am courting Miss Elizabeth."

"What is this you say? Courting Miss Elizabeth? How is this possible?" Bingley choked on his coffee. "Mr. Collins told me *he* was courting her."

"He is." Darcy grinned at the confused look on Bingley's face. The whole situation really was odd. "You should know, my friend, that if you choose to pursue Miss Jane Bennet, you will be dealing with a very crafty father who not only wants the best for his daughters, he is not above provoking sport for his own entertainment."

At Bingley's blush, Darcy knew his friend's affections for the eldest Bennet were sincere. What Darcy was not prepared for was Bingley's response.

"How well I know, Darcy," Bingley placed his utensils on his plate. "While you and Mr. Collins have been spending time in competition, I have been meeting Jane in the garden in full view of Mrs. Bennet and Miss Mary. Where you only get thirty minutes to achieve your goals, I am allowed the full hour. So, I thank you, my friend, for distracting said father. I am considering requesting a courtship by the time Mr. Collins leaves for Kent. I am already thinking of our engagement and marriage as well, though I am in no hurry to rush into matrimony. Miss Bennet, my Jane, is an angel. I believe I could search the world and fine no one else who matches me in temperament. She is the one for me."

"Bingley!" Darcy was stunned. "You sly fox."

INSIDE LONGBOURN, Mrs. Bennet loudly proclaimed her pleasure at having the Netherfield party as guests. Mr. Collins stood alongside her with his hands on his lapels as if he was solely responsible for the Mistress of Longbourn's happiness.

Elizabeth started to walk by Darcy as if she was not going to acknowledge him only to have her grab his arm and pull him from the drawing room. One glance at her face was enough to know she had reached her limit. Her cheeks were rosy, her lips were pressed together until they were white, and her eyes shot fire.

Gathering their outer clothes, they stepped outside.

"Pardon me, Mr. Darcy. I need a moment."

Standing on the steps, she closed her eyes and inhaled deeply three times. Letting out the last breath slowly, she held her hands out, palms facing down, lowering them until they were relaxed at her side.

Figuring the wisest course was silence, he offered his arm and they began to walk.

The rain had come the day before. The air was damp, and puddles littered the lane. Within minutes, it became a challenge to find a path where they would not be soaked from head to feet.

"This is not my best idea," she mentioned as they were caught walking single-file between two water-filled ruts the carriages returning from worship had made deeper. "Perhaps we should, instead, spend a quiet half hour in my father's study."

What? Court in front of her father? Pray, not!

"Certainly, if that is what you prefer," he said instead.

His internal sigh was heartfelt. "However, I have another suggestion, if you please?"

Gazing up at him, she lifted her brows, an expression that always made him smile.

"Mightn't we walk the garden paths instead? I have it from my friend that there we will be under your mother's supervision rather than your father's. In fact, since Mr. Bennet was in the drawing room and not his private refuge, we would be properly chaperoned by them both."

"A brilliant idea, sir." Leading him around the side of the house, they strolled towards the rose garden where wisteria trellises remained covered with some greenery.

"I do have a question for you, Miss Elizabeth," he paused until she nodded. "Why is it your mother appears to approve of Mr. Collins' pursuit over mine? As a mother of five living in an entailed estate, I had assumed her preference would be for the man who was in a better position to aid your family financially. Yet, she has yet to extend assistance to me, unlike what she has done for both Mr. Collins and Bingley. Have I done something to anger her?"

"Mr. Darcy, that you care for the opinion of my mother is quite the surprise, you who have only held her previously in disdain." Elizabeth halted and looked back at her house. Sure enough, Mrs. Bennet and Mr. Collins stood at the window and watched them. "Is it that you care more for why she is not giving you aid to help your own cause, or do you truly want to know the workings of her mind?"

"While I freely admit that I do not understand this situation, I genuinely want to know."

"As a matter of interest, sir, I too wondered at Mama pushing me towards Mr. Collins since it was she who informed our whole family and many of the neighbors about your estimated income. Other than being the heir to Longbourn, Mr. Collins has little of monetary value, as I understand."

"Ten thousand a year is, in truth, lower than my yearly average."

She nodded but gave no clue that she was impressed by his annual revenue. "My mother wants the best for each one of her daughters, of this I have no doubt. Therefore, I am perplexed at her favorable opinion of our father's cousin. He is a silly man with little intelligence. I wonder if it was merely because his offer came first."

"I cannot know," he said. "I can assume then that her motives are not mercenary. That her attachment to Longbourn is the reason? Would I be correct?"

"This, I can answer." With her hand around his elbow, she turned him to face the building. "I will agree that some of my mother's concerns are about the security of herself and her children. Nonetheless, when you look at Longbourn, you likely see a smallish stone building filled with females sitting on well-farmed acreage. My mother sees a home she created over the years, since the days she arrived as a new bride. Proudly displayed in each room are artwork and artifacts from each of her children. She gave birth to all five of us here. Two years after Lydia was born, she was delivered of my brother, James. He did not survive the week. My mother almost did not as well. Little James is buried in the cemetery next to Longbourn chapel. Therefore, Longbourn represents much more to her than a place to live out the rest of her years. It is memories created and cherished. Love gained and lost. It is a foundation laid for her life together with my father. To leave here would be to leave that life and those memories behind. Do you understand?"

"I do." Easily envisioned were his many memories at Pemberley, all of them more precious than his wealth. Having his parents entombed in the chapel grounds would forever tie his heart to the property. The loss of these memories would be devastating. "Are you as tied to Longbourn?"

"No, as it is different for a female child." They resumed walking. "My girlhood memories are of the people, more than the building. This is important because part of growing up is knowing how small a percentage of our lifetime will be spent here. Once we are established elsewhere, then our personal moments with the family a new wife helps develop becomes the focal point of her existence. Then, she will store away and cherish treasured remembrances to take out later when her own children are gone."

He felt her explanation in the depths of his heart. "I comprehend your meaning, and I thank you sincerely for your having shared this with me. Now that her two eldest daughters are being courted with the intentions of marriage; your mother is pondering having each of her children leave her nest until only your father remains. Should he not survive her, to lose him and her home at the same time would be truly devastating."

"Yes, Mr. Darcy, this very much is my mother's reality. As each day passes, she becomes more frantic at suffering each of those losses. Because of this, her attitude is skewed until her only desire is to grab ahold of the only thing that would keep matters as they are."

"I would offer Mr. Collins a small fortune, enough to purchase another estate should he desire, to deed Longbourn to her." And, he would, if necessary.

Elizabeth squeezed his arm. "I am beginning to believe you might be a good man, Mr. Darcy."

CHAPTER 8

The next morning, he woke to pouring rain. There would be no walking out with Elizabeth on that day. The time remaining before her decision would be made was speeding by, and Darcy felt he had little progress to show for the passing minutes. Yet, in reality, that was not exactly the case. Elizabeth had smiled at him, three times—genuine expressions of appreciation and joy. And, her final comment he would take as a compliment to him. That she considered he *might* be a good man was tremendous progress from the start when she loathed him.

Used to being greeted by a frustrated Elizabeth, he was surprised when she met him at the door with a slight grin that looked ninety-nine parts mischief and one small part sweet. He had no clue what was on her mind. She seemed particularly reluctant to share.

They were seated in Mr. Bennet's study, a chessboard between them. Mr. Bennet was reading, or at least he was giving the appearance of doing so. The quiet was broken by the snap and crackle of the logs in the fireplace. The setting was cozy. The air was warm as calmness added to Darcy's contentment. He could easily picture days spent in the same activity at Pemberley once she agreed to wed him. Well, without Mr. Bennet's presence, of course.

Within minutes of starting the game, Darcy comprehended her pleasure. Elizabeth had been taught well. Her skill at chess was equal or perhaps superior to his. What a delight!

But that was not the only reason she was in a happy mood.

"Sir, do you recall that I mentioned we had a spy at Longbourn?"

Darcy saw Mr. Bennet's head snap to attention at her comment. However, the man said nothing, merely rested his book on his lap before giving his total focus to Elizabeth.

"I do. Did someone somehow discover the chocolates Georgiana had delivered to you?"

"They did," she could no longer contain her mirth. "Unfortunately, or rather, fortunately, Mr. Collins immediately took his pony cart to Meryton to discover if any treats were being offered at the haberdashery. He must have found a treasure trove of them."

"Were they as tasty as the ones from London?" He wanted them *not* to be.

"I would not know." At the quizzical expression that must have appeared on his face, she continued, "The weather, as my father and you predicted, turned poorly before he arrived back at Longbourn. Rather than have the rain damage the package with the sweets, Mr. Collins stuffed them all in his mouth as the storm reached its peak. By the time he arrived at the front door, his face was pale, his cheeks were still bulging, he was soaked from head to toe, and he was unable to swallow the mass in his mouth."

"Oh, no," he readily joined Mr. Bennet and Elizabeth's laughter. What a picture her description made.

She added, "I will not share the mess our housekeeper was confronted with. However, I will confess that Mr. Collins made a pretty little apology some hours later."

Time passed as mutual hilarity relaxed the three in the study. All Darcy could think of was, "poor Mr. Collins." He had no idea he had said it aloud until Mr. Bennet spoke.

"Mr. Darcy," Elizabeth's father blurted into the silence. "We are expecting a guest to arrive any moment who claims an acquaintance with you. I would hope the interruption to your 'courting' will not be a disappointment."

Darcy was immediately on alert. With Wickham gone from Hertfordshire, he could not imagine who would feel the need to travel to Meryton, except...*Oh, good Lord!* Lady Catherine. That fool preacher must have written her about the circumstances of the competition. *Idiot!*

Endeavoring to rein in his emotions, Darcy responded, "Is Mrs. Bennet aware she is expecting a stranger?"

"She will find out soon enough," Mr. Bennet gleefully replied. Looking out the window, he added, "Might her horses be four matching bays?"

"She is here," Darcy whispered under his breath. Without thought, he grabbed Elizabeth's hand which had just picked up a pawn. Looking her straight in the eye, he said, "Pray, do not hold anything that comes out of her mouth against me or Georgiana. If Mr. Collins has told her of my part in this courtship, her vitriol against you will be particularly sharp. I shall do all in my power to protect you."

"You will, will you? How?" was her quick response. Her spine had stiffened as she jerked her hand from his.

He was confused, no longer on solid ground. "You are asking how I aim to guard you, is that correct?"

Darcy knew his question was stupid, but he could not wrap his mind around a female who would not jump at the chance of having someone speak and act for her against his aunt. With that thought, he had a brilliant idea. "Perhaps it would be best should you remain in your father's study. As soon as she leaves, I will return to you without fail."

From the corner of his eye, Darcy spotted Mr. Bennet shaking his head, while looking directly at him. Thus, he missed Elizabeth's expression before she jumped up from her chair.

He stood as well.

"Mr. Darcy, if you think..." she began, her tone as sharp as a blade.

Mr. Bennet broke in. "Children, no fighting." Again, he gazed out the window. "The carriage has stopped. Lady Catherine shall soon enter Longbourn. I suggest you come to terms with how you mean to proceed in as few minutes as possible. I shall leave you to your discussion."

Sheer frustration warred with worry. How could he get Elizabeth to understand he wanted only what would be best for her? Darcy yearned to keep her from the verbal nonsense he knew was to come. Lady Catherine rarely used restraint when she was upset. In fact, never in his memory could he recall her using tact.

Putting his palm over his mouth, Darcy wondered, was he using tact? No, he was not. Therefore, he began again. "Elizabeth, you have heard my suggestion for how to best deal with my aunt. Do you have another recommendation you would like to share? I would be pleased to hear what you have to offer."

When her right brow rose almost to her hairline, he suspected he had done well.

Without hesitation she answered, "I shall not be left behind. I will stand at your side, or I will not stand with you at all. Ever!"

"Then, I will tell you, Elizabeth Bennet, that my confidence rises at any attempt to intimidate me." He stepped around the small game table to stand inches from her. "I am not afraid of my aunt. I never have been. I am master of Pemberley and guardian of Georgiana. Lady Catherine has no authority over me." He moved inches closer. "I do, however, fear displeasing you. I am also deeply in love with you—so in love that I want you, and no one else, by my side until I take my final breath on this earth."

She was direct in her attitude. "I imagine you believe what you say, sir, which is a good thing since you have not hidden your goal of offering marriage to me and having me accept. Yet, you must by now realize that arrogance and pride are abhorrent to me. I hope you have learned to temper these qualities enough that I can see the true Mr. Darcy, especially under trial?"

"You are certain you will not remain behind?" Looking her over from head to toe, he saw a warrior instead of a meek, submissive, pale specimen of a woman. "Yes, I can see that you are."

"I will tell you clearly, sir, that how you treat this situation with your aunt, my parents, Mr. Collins, and myself will tell me more about your inner character than a multitude of thirty-minute periods."

Good heavens! Did she expect him to be amiable when she was in the line of fire? He would do anything for her. But this? Well, he would certainly try.

His eyes moved to where she was biting the corner of her lower lip. He longed to stop her abuse, tenderly caressing her mouth with his own. But the time was not right.

Lowering her gaze from his, giving him no clue to her thoughts or feelings, she stepped to his side, wrapping her hand around his elbow. "Then, let us proceed into the fray."

* * *

THE SCENE in the drawing room was not inviting. Lady Catherine was seated in Mrs. Bennet's normal chair. Mr. Collins hovered over her. Mr. and Mrs. Bennet were across from them. Bingley and Jane had tucked themselves away in a distant corner, although they would still be witness to the confrontation. The younger girls had fled.

When Darcy and Elizabeth arrived, Lady Catherine stood and approached. Her lackey followed.

"This," she pointed her walking stick at Elizabeth. "This is the girl who deigns to step into my sister's shoes as mistress of Pemberley? Why, she is nothing to look at. My word, Fitzwilliam. She has freckles on her nose and her hair is as dark as night. What can you be thinking? She will never do as your wife." Walking slowly around them, Lady Catherine kept up her commentary. "This chit is good enough for Collins but you, you deserve a lady rich in assets and personality like my Anne."

He gritted his teeth hard as he struggled to be the man that he thought Elizabeth wanted. As he said nothing, his fingers pushed into his palm, so tight was his fist. Mr. Collins remained silent as well.

Darcy might have been able to maintain control had his aunt not finished her tirade with, "No, this baggage will never do for a Darcy."

Scarlett red flooded his vision. He was done being nice. Looking at Elizabeth, he pleaded, "My dear, I want to be the gentleman you admire and trust. I walked into this room next to you as you desired. I want to be calm. I long to be humble so you no longer find me arrogant. However, I am, indeed, a proud man. I am proud of my willingness to work hard for those I love and care for. I am proud of the name I hope to share with you one day. I am proud of Georgiana for recognizing your value far quicker than I. Mostly, I am proud of you, that you stand solidly for your beliefs and for what is right. Because of this, I can no longer remain silent. Do not ask it of me, I pray you."

"I will not ask it of you, sir." It was in her eyes, kindness and acceptance.

He stepped in front of Elizabeth, using his right hand to guide her behind him. Then he approached his aunt. "You have said quite enough, Madam." Using his height, he loomed over her, his pose every inch intimidating. "How dare you use filth to describe a woman so rare and precious to me. You have overstepped all that is proper by coming here to interfere in a matter unrelated to you in an attempt to change my mind. I have told you many times that I will never marry Anne. You do not listen. You have wasted your time and are wasting mine."

"Bah!" Lady Catherine rapped her walking stick on the floor. "Look at you. A Darcy competing for a simple country girl's affection against a lowly clergyman. Is she lacking in understanding? Does she have no intelligence? Does she not know who you are? And you, Fitzwilliam? What sort of arts and allurements has she used to trap you? Was there a compromise? Did you display human weakness in the face of her blatant pursuit? If so, it is of no matter. Collins and she can quickly wed. I will arrange for your by-blow to be shipped off to a workhouse, so you are not bothered. Then, Collins can read the banns for you and Anne. You will take her home to Pemberley before the year ends. All will be as it should be."

"No!" Darcy's voice quieted to almost a whisper, forcing Lady Catherine and Mr. Collins to lean towards him. "Take heed, the both of you. I will never see Elizabeth married to anyone other than myself. Ever! If I need to spend a lifetime earning her regard, I will do so."

The dream he had after the Netherfield ball haunted him. It was then he understood just how far he was willing to go to secure Elizabeth Bennet as his wife.

His smile unnerved Lady Catherine. Ignoring Mr. Collins, he bowed to her alone. She was sputtering when he held up his palm for silence.

"Lady Catherine, your purpose is doomed to fail. You are finished here." He turned his back to his aunt, in effect, giving her the cut direct. Returning to Elizabeth, he gently took her hand in his, bringing her fingers to his lips as he continued to address his aunt. "Because of you, I now know how far I am willing to go to have Elizabeth for my bride. I will change what I need to change. I will become whatever and whomever I need to be her husband. The only one who can stop me is Elizabeth. She alone holds the key to my heart and soul. You have as much power as a lion with its teeth and claws removed."

"Humph!" His aunt stalked around where he stood with Elizabeth. "You have made your offer then?"

"I have not."

"Then, you will not!" his aunt insisted, rapping her cane on the floor with each word.

"I am resolved to act in that manner, which will, in my own opinion, constitute my happiness, without reference to you, or to any person whether connected to me or not. Therefore, I shall make my proposal as often as possible until she finally says 'yes'."

"I take no leave of you, Fitzwilliam. You deserve no such attention. I am most seriously displeased."

When she stomped out of the door, those remaining in the room were frozen in place. Nevertheless, their facial expressions revealed much.

Mr. Collins appeared to be greatly put out that his beloved patroness had not helped him carry his point. He would *not* be marrying Elizabeth. Bingley and Jane were still in the corner, whispering between themselves. Mr. Bennet had reached for his wife's hand, whether to offer her comfort or to gain such, Darcy did not know.

Nonetheless, it was his Elizabeth whose response pleased him the most.

"Mr. Darcy, I believe we need to talk."

He could not agree more.

Looking out the window, he noted a break in the weather.

"We have yet to walk the lane today. I still have thirty minutes, I believe, if you are willing?" Tucking her hand inside his own, he was pleased with her reply.

"I am willing." Then, she smiled.

CHAPTER 9

Lady Catherine's carriage was pulling away when the couple stepped out of the front door. From habit, Darcy checked the time on his pocket watch.

"Well, sir, I think that went quite well," she chuckled.

He laughed in relief at her quip.

"Only you, Elizabeth." He offered his arm, basically assured of her acceptance. There was a small measure of consolation as soon as he felt her hand rest where it belonged. "Might I ask, or would it be too much, for an explanation of your comment?"

She grinned. "Are you referring to my statement that we needed to talk or that I am willing?"

"I would say both."

"From the start, Mr. Darcy, you were made aware of the two qualities needed to capture my heart. Do you recall?

"I do." They began walking down the lane. "Respect and affection."

"Yes." She looked at him as she moved beside him. "My hope was to have a marriage where love was forged so strong that nothing would move us, shake us, or break us. In listening to you stand up for the two of us to your aunt, I finally realized that together we could be formidable."

"A formidable marriage," he mused. "I do like the sound of it, Elizabeth."

"As do I," she agreed happily. "During our half hour periods, you gave me a choice to have quiet when I could tell you wanted to speak. You asked my way despite wanting your own way. And you did not ask me to share my chocolate sweets. To me, that is the mark of a true gentleman, one I might like to attach myself to for a lifetime."

He could walk no farther.

"Do you love me, Elizabeth?"

The corners of her eyes crinkled as her nose twitched. "I do believe you are growing on me...Fitzwilliam."

What was a man to do? Cupping her face, he lowered his lips to hers. After two more kisses, he whispered, "Marry me?"

"I just might," she breathed her reply. "I believe between now and the wedding day I will become agreeable to the task."

He was the happiest man on earth. Miss Elizabeth Bennet would become Mrs. Darcy, his beloved, forever.

"I need to speak to your father." He pulled away, recalling where they were and that Mr. Bennet was undoubtedly watching them closely. As the guardian of a young girl, he knew how he would feel should a gentleman display his affections prior to asking permission.

He groaned. "Will he torment me over this?"

"Most likely," she grinned. "But do not worry. If my father has seen us, so has my mother. She will make absolutely certain she has a son-to-be before the day is out."

"Then, bless Mrs. Bennet."

Happily, they walked hand and hand back to Longbourn. Darcy never knew such joy—the joy that was *his* Elizabeth.

ONE MONTH later -

"Miss Elizabeth Bennet, wilt thou have this man to be thy wedded husband, to live together after God's ordinance in the holy estate of Matrimony? Wilt thou obey him, and serve him, love, honor, and keep him, in sickness and in health; and, forsaking all other, keep thee only unto him, so long as ye both shall live?"

Darcy's breath was stuck somewhere in his throat as he awaited her reply. Finally, after mischief filled her expression, she said, "Yes, I will".

He did not recall exhaling in relief until after they both recited their vows.

Within a few short moments, they were pronounced man and wife.

In the weeks leading up to their wedding, he had shared the vivid account of his nightmare with Elizabeth. She had first sympathized, then became indignant at being tossed over his shoulder as he had stomped out of the chapel. Then, she kissed away the remnants of his memories, replacing them with her promise that she would marry him and no other.

There had been many times during their official engagement that he had yearned to toss her into his carriage and head to Scotland. Mrs. Bennet had staunch ideas of the extensive preparations for the wedding. Bingley's sisters made his stay at Netherfield Park miserable as they learned quickly not to speak publicly, especially to him, about the qualifications of any of the Bennet daughters to be a society bride. Occasionally, Mr. Collins would write, as did Lady Catherine, letters filled with threats and disappointments.

It was a pleasure to have Anne de Bourgh in attendance for the ceremony, accompanied by his Fitzwilliam relatives. Her support meant much to both Darcy and Elizabeth.

Miss Georgiana Darcy loved her new sister from the moment they met. She also found much in common with Miss Jane Bennet. Within hours, they became fast friends. During the wedding breakfast, Georgiana informed her brother that she wanted to remain at Longbourn during their wedding journey rather than impose on the new bride and groom. Neither Darcy nor Elizabeth minded the idea of being alone, which was exactly where they wanted to be.

Mr. Bennet had taken a liking to the young Miss Darcy, feeling it was his responsibility to tell her the tale of one bride and two grooms. Georgiana replied with a boldness that surprised Darcy of her own part in the scheme. From that point on, she would be forever welcomed at Longbourn.

When the newly wedded couple was ready to depart for their northern destination of Pemberley, Mr. Bennet took Darcy aside.

"I am proud to have you as my son, Darcy." Mr. Bennet slapped him companionably on the shoulder. "Take good care of my girl, and do not be a stranger to us."

"I swear with my life that I will do as you ask, Bennet." Darcy paused before asking what weighed heaviest on his mind. Finally, he spoke his concerns aloud. "Do you believe Elizabeth chose the correct groom?"

"Beyond a shadow of a doubt." Mr. Bennet chuckled. "You were always my choice."

Grateful he had his new family's support; Darcy gathered his wife and left Longbourn.

As they entered the carriage, Darcy thought, *one bride plus one groom* (himself)—*perfect!*

EPILOGUE

Mr. Bennet moved to where his wife stood watching the couple out the front window. The newlywed's hands were joined. Their heads were tilted towards each other as they stopped before stepping into the carriage. When Mr. Darcy took her face in his hands, Elizabeth's father knew what was coming. He looked away.

"We did it, Mr. Bennet," his wife of almost twenty-five years patted his hand where it rested on the sill.

"That we did, dearest." He chuckled. "I would never have known two such stubborn people would be the perfect match. You are positively brilliant, my bride."

She blushed. "No, dear. I do appreciate the compliment, but this time it is undeserved."

"How so, Blossom?"

She smirked. "As he watched Lizzy, I watched him. Then I spoke extensively with Mr. Bingley to determine his true character. I will admit the charm of Mr. Wickham almost had me changing my mind. Nevertheless, one whisper from Mrs. Morton at the inn in Meryton convinced me one was a gentleman while the other had only the appearance of being moral. I was convinced that true love would result if we could convince both Darcy and Lizzy of each other's character."

"My wife, I will admit I almost choked when Lizzy spoke with our new son about there being a spy in the house. By the by, our Lizzy still believes it to be Lydia."

"Silly girls!" Mrs. Bennet grinned. "They all think they know what is going on with their parents and are convinced we do nothing other than fret over them."

He laughed, hugging her to him. "You did well, my dear."

"We did, did we not?" she replied.

"Then our work is done." Mr. Bennet was exceedingly satisfied with the outcome. He both admired and respected Mr. Darcy and was grateful his second daughter now felt the same.

"Not quite." Mrs. Bennet left the window to sit by the fire. Guests were beginning to gather their outer garments and follow the Darcy's example. However, there were still neighbors and friends wanting to socialize in the old ballroom they had opened for the wedding celebration. She knew she and her husband would not be missed for a bit.

"Mrs. Bennet, are you scheming again?" Her husband followed.

"Well, Mr. Collins was unknowingly of great assistance to our purpose in attaching Darcy to Lizzy, my dear. He is still at Longbourn, is he not?"

"He is, much to my chagrin," Mr. Bennet shook his

head in disappointment. Lady Catherine had sent her parson back to Hertfordshire in a last-minute effort to halt the Darcy wedding. Mr. Collins had failed spectacularly. "And you are enquiring because...?"

"By any chance, did Mr. Bingley come up to snuff and ask for Jane's hand this morning before the wedding?"

"He did not." Suddenly, he could see where his wife's mind had traveled. "Are you thinking a word to my cousin would put him on the path to Jane now that Lizzy is quite unavailable?"

"Mr. Bennet, unlike the seven days I gave you for Mr. Collins to push Mr. Darcy towards the correct decision, I believe it would take less than a day for Mr. Bingley."

"Hah!" he chortled. "I say less than a half a day."

"Hmmm!" she mused. "Two brides and two grooms."

"We are not counting Mr. Collins, I see," he snorted.

"Absolutely not!" Mrs. Bennet insisted. "Mr. Bennet, you may have won the last time we bet as it was exactly five days from the beginning of Darcy's courtship to his proposal. To be fair, you are probably correct about Mr. Bingley." Standing, she moved to the drawing room doorway. "Nevertheless, I gladly accept your wager. May the best one of us win."

"I assume you expect it to be yourself this time?"

"Perhaps. Perhaps not."

"When should we inform Mr. and Mrs. Darcy about our 'arranging' their courtship?"

"My dear, Mr. Bennet. We should say nothing until only the two of us remain at Longbourn. We may need to utilize Mr. Collins' unwitting service again in the future for the rest of our girls. We would not want anything or anyone, including the Darcys, to interfere with our plans, would we?"

Before, she completely left the room, they turned back to the window to see Mr. Darcy's carriage slowly moving down the lane. Despite the joy of the occasion, both were feeling melancholy.

He said, "Mrs. Bennet, should any other eligible men appear interested in Mary, Kitty, or Lydia, please send them in. I am quite at my leisure."

The End

FROM THE AUTHOR:

Christie Capps is the pen name of a best-selling author J Dawn King who, because of increasing demands on her time, has fewer and fewer hours to read. She doubts she is the only one with these circumstances. Therefore, her Christie Capps stories will all be approximately 100 pages of sweet romance and will be priced less than one cup of flavored coffee from your local barista.

Happy reading!

ALREADY AVAILABLE - FROM CHRISTIE CAPPS

Mr. Darcy's Bad Day
For Pemberley
The Perfect Gift
A Forever Kind of Love
Boxed Set: Something Old, New, Later, True
Elizabeth
Lost and Found
Henry
His Frozen Heart
Boxed Set: Something Regency, Romantic, Rollicking & Reflective
One Bride & Two Grooms
A Reason to Hope
Mischief & Mayhem
The Matchmaker
Boxed Set: Something Priceless, Perilous, Precious & Playful

ALREADY AVAILABLE - FROM J DAWN KING:

Mr. Darcy's Mail-Order Bride

Love Letters from Mr. Darcy

The Abominable Mr. Darcy

Yes, Mr. Darcy

Compromised!

A Father's Sins

One Love - Two Hearts - Three Loves

A Baby for Mr. Darcy

Friends and Enemies

The Letter of the Law

A Long Journey Home

Mistaken Identity

Field Of Dreams

THANK YOU VERY MUCH!

I sincerely appreciate you for investing your time with this story. A gift for any author is to receive an honest review from readers. I hope you will use this opportunity to let others know your opinion of this tale. Happy reading!

Made in the USA
Middletown, DE
27 August 2023

37240237R00059